Bernard J Snell

Gain or Loss

An Appreciation of the Results of Recent Biblical Criticism

Bernard J Snell

Gain or Loss
An Appreciation of the Results of Recent Biblical Criticism

ISBN/EAN: 9783742810090

Manufactured in Europe, USA, Canada, Australia, Japa

Cover: Foto ©Andreas Hilbeck / pixelio.de

Manufactured and distributed by brebook publishing software
(www.brebook.com)

Bernard J Snell

Gain or Loss

GAIN OR LOSS?

AN APPRECIATION OF THE RESULTS OF
RECENT BIBLICAL CRITICISM.

BY THE REV.

BERNARD J. SNELL,

M.A., B.Sc.

*Five Lectures delivered at Brixton Independent
Church, London.*

London:

JAMES CLARKE & CO., 13 & 14, FLEET STREET.

—

1895.

First Edition, *March, 1895.*

Second Edition, *April, 1895.*

PREFACE.

IT is an old winter custom at Brixton Independent Church for the minister to announce a series of Sunday Evening Lectures for the continuous treatment of one theme. In response to many suggestions, I undertook this subject, I trust with a due sense of responsibility; and with some hesitation, I have consented to the publication of the Lectures. They will be regarded as commonplace by many students of Biblical Criticism, and as a superfluous attempt to do poorly what has been done by others with conspicuous ability. But

it must be remembered, in ex-
tenuation of my offence, that
the pews of our churches are
filled with unceasing relays of
young men and women to whom
it is more difficult than ever to
hold the Faith of Christ in the
old forms. For their sake I
spoke, and for their sake this
little volume is printed, in the
hope that I may help some to
maintain an intelligent hold of
those Truths

" Which, be they what they may,
Are yet the fountain-light of all our day,
    Are yet a master-light of all our seeing ;
Uphold us, cherish, and have power to make
    Our noisy years seem moments in the
        being
Of the Eternal Silence ; truths that wake,
        To perish never."

CONTENTS.

I.

A PLEA FOR FREE INQUIRY.

A PLEA FOR FREE INQUIRY.

"Ye shall know the truth, and the truth shal make you free."—St. John viii. 32.

THE highest reverence for the Bible is shown when we take it simply as it stands, and try to learn what it means. That is true criticism. To say that it is presumption to criticise the Bible shows an utter misunderstanding of the idea. For criticism is not merely depreciatory and privative : criticism is judgment, appreciation. All study is criticism. The Bible is not the one book which we are forbidden to taste, or to presume to understand. On the contrary, if there is a book in the world to be read with eyes open, it is the Bible. The Bible has a

meaning like every other book,
its meaning is to be discovered
in the same way. We shall not
love the Bible less, if we scru-
tinise it more. It is futile to
claim that these sacred records
will stand the same scrutiny as
secular records, unless the claim
can be guaranteed by the same
tests. Men have too long been
invited to accept the Bible for
ultra-rational reasons; it is time
to base the appeal on rational
reasons. Talk about "not coming to the Bible with our
reason"—it is the only way we
can come.

There is no let or hindrance
in the Religion of Christ to the
pursuit of truth, nor is there
any Christian virtue involved
in resolutely refusing to change
the opinion we have held.
Inquiry after truth cannot be
displeasing to the God of truth.
All inquiry is safe while we
keep our eyes towards the light

and our feet in the path of duty.
It is not a matter of faith who
wrote the Psalms or who edited
the Hexateuch; it is a matter for
legitimate inquiry. So far from
ignorance being the mother of
devotion, ignorance and prejudice are among the greatest
obstacles to the coming of the
Kingdom. Those who value
the Bible will take pains to
understand it.

I am persuaded that the truly
orthodox view of the Bible is
that view which holds most of
the facts, and that the Bible
becomes ever more beautiful,
more vitally historical and spiritually significant the more
we understand it. The higher
critics are not the latest ene-
mies of Revelation—unbeliev-
ers over whom we should utter
jeremiads, and at whose names
we should start with alarm.
They are scholars who for
devout love of the Scriptures

prosecute, after a scientific method, the study of all the facts to hand. If their conclusions are wrong, only better scholarship than theirs can prove them so.

If the true meaning of Scripture can be obtained, there is some hope of general agreement among men ; and there is a manifest tendency on the part of critics to find common ground. It is sometimes said that the religion of all sensible men is the same. If, then, all sensible men can be induced to agree as to the plain meaning of Scripture, to that degree there is hope of a diminution of those lamentable sects and schisms which have arisen largely from divergencies of interpretation. The lines of separation will vanish, when once the spiritual becomes transcendent, all in all.

While some oscillate between superstitious idolatry of the

book and its total rejection, there are many, unable to entertain the traditional view of the Bible, who want to save their faith without slaying their intelligence. There is a smouldering scepticism, the extent of which is realised by few. Parents say, "We cannot read the Bible to our children, for we cannot answer their questions." And I am bound to do my best to help you read the Bible without equivocation, to help you retain for yourselves and your children the substance of the faith, and keep a way open for Religion in your hearts. Without a sure foundation Faith crumbles before the first attack.

There is always a danger and temptation to a preacher to become petty in his treatment of the Bible. The authorities, whom he consults, have weighed the exact force of each word of

the original by the finest mea-
surement, and many of them
under a sense that eternal destiny hung on the result. And
grammatical construction has
been insisted on to a degree
which almost justifies the re-
mark of Matthew Arnold upon
the translators of the Revised
Version, that they "seemed to
think that man was made for
the aorist and not the aorist for
man." But all, save the blind, can
see that there is danger in the
alienation between the best current scholarship and Christian
activities, and that here lies the
source of much popular indiffer-
ence and scepticism. The story
of past civilisation warns us
that a bridge is needed between
the thoughts of the scholars
and popular faith, or the gulf
will widen till Religion itself is
swallowed up. You want to
teach your children the truth
and nothing but the truth, at

the same time that you teach
them Religion. It is a perilous
experiment to separate the two.
Suppose you are very anxious
that your boy should not spill
the ink, and you tell him that
the inkstand stings. You certainly succeed in inducing him
to avoid it. But on the day on
which he discovers that it does
not sting, his confidence in you
is undermined. Teach your lad
that the Bible is *verbatim et
literatim* the very Word of God,
and for a time your method
succeeds; but one day he will
find, as you have done, mistakes
and incongruities, and he will
turn to you with the just indig-
nation of a young man, and say,
"I wanted the truth, and you
taught me falsehood." Men and
brethren, the claim of Biblical
infallibility is a ghost with
which you can coerce children;
but children grow up to dis-
believe in ghosts.

In view of these facts I recognise the duty of speaking as plainly as I can and of answering any real questions, in order that I may show our religion to be in harmony with the results of historical criticism, as it is in harmony with the verified results of natural research, and in order that I may, if possible, blend the best results of current scholarship with the old reverence of the faithful. Of course, I am no specialist in the exploration of the documents that lie so close to the faith of Christendom. But I have gathered information from all quarters, principally from the English scholars, into the fruits of whose labours we have entered—Robertson Smith, Driver, Cheyne. I have consulted many books in general currency, like Miss Wedgwood's "Message of Israel," and Dr. Horton's "Revelation and the Bible," which

try to hand on in popular
form for general consumption
the conclusions of the experts,
so that my indebtedness and
research have been somewhat
widespread. But I shall be
rewarded if I succeed in bring-
ing the words of Christ a little
nearer to your hearts, and in
making that great Son of Man
stand out in finer sublimity
as the Lord of Life. "These
things are written that ye may
believe, and that believing ye
may have life."

It is a shock to many intelligent believers to hear what are
the results of the ripest erudi-
tion applied to the problem of
the Bible :—that Hebrew literature did not begin before the
ninth century B.C. ; that Moses
did not write the Pentateuch,
nor David the Psalms ; that
the major part of the Judaic
Law was delivered, not amid
the thunders of Sinai, but

to a nameless innovator in
Babylon a millennium after ;
that the Books of the Law, so
far from being homogeneous,
are the composite product of
many documents under several
editors, and were introduced by
Ezra only 444 years B.C. ; that
the Psalms are five Temple
Hymn-books joined together,
most of them dating from the
time of the Maccabees ; that
Solomon did not write Ecclesiastes, nor The Song, nor The
Proverbs ; that Isaiah wrote
only half the book that bears his
name ; that Jeremiah wrote not
all of " Jeremiah," and none of
Lamentations ; that Daniel did
not write a word of " Daniel,"
and Zechariah only a part of
"Zechariah " ; that only half of
the Old Testament was written
before the Exile ; that Ezekiel
is earlier than the Levitical
legislation, and Deuteronomy
of the age of King Josiah ; that

in the New Testament many books are moved from their traditional anchorage : that Paul did not write the Epistle to the Hebrews, and that his authorship of the pastoral Epistles to Timothy and Titus is questioned ; that the Second Epistle of St. Peter is non-Petrine ; that though the fourth Gospel may be genuinely derived from St. John, there are interlinear additions by a later hand, and that the present form was not assumed till the beginning of the second century.

Now, it is not surprising that the bare list of such readjustment of names and dates should excite some uneasiness, nor that some should go trembling for the Ark of God. But let us remember that to entertain fear of truth is distinctly dishonouring to the God of truth. Let us nourish the steadfast confidence that truth is strong and will

prevail. We are born for truth,
and truth must be better than
mistakes. "Things are what
they are, and the results will
be what they will be." Danger
arises only when we deny truth;
the only safety for the Bible is in
telling the truth about it. No
fraud is more mischievous than
pious fraud; the call to be
religious is not stronger than
the call to see of what sort our
religion is, and it may be
necessary to exorcise a superstition to save a truth. Nothing
can invalidate a proved fact;
and criticism, by restoring these
books to their original form, has
really restored to them a higher
authority. Christianity no more
falls to pieces, because we learn
the truth about the Bible, than
the stars fall when you fold
up your telescope.

To say that the Bible must be
approached on the same footing
as other books by no means

implies that they are its equals;
any more than to say that we
must come to a painting by
Rembrandt and a work of an
unknown artist in the same
mental posture, implies that
they are of equal artistic value.
A man who has just been helped
and made anew by the Bible is
apt to say, "That Book which
made a new man of me does
not contain a single flaw; I
will test with it everything
beside; I will ascertain from it
whether our astronomers tell
us the truth, whether adders
are deaf or conies chew the
cud; what it says I will hold
to." Now, that is hardly final
as against the zoological facts
that conies do not chew the cud,
and that adders have auditory
nerves. Questions of fact, of
history and philology, cannot be
decided by the most devout of
presumptions in favour of the
plenary authority of Scripture.

Such an attitude cannot stand
against the conclusions of
scholarship any more than
the plucky Matabeles could
stand against our magazine
rifles.

Did God Almighty dictate
one view of a king's life and
character to one writer, and
another to another? Did He
furnish to Moses one summary
of the history of the captivity
of Israel in Egypt, and of the
Exodus, and of the giving of
the Law, and quite an incon-
sistent summary to St. Stephen?
Did God lead the first three
Evangelists to describe the last
meal taken by Christ as the
true Jewish Passover, while
He led the fourth Evangelist
to describe the Last Supper
as eaten on the day before
the Jewish Passover? Can
such an incredible view of Inspiration be endorsed? "Mys-
tery"! It is mystification; and

there is no more wholesome
discipline in trying to crowd
such incongruities into the
mind, than there is in trying
to believe that seven times six
is other than six times seven.
It is simply intellectual confusion.

"Oh, bother the scholars!"
says the plain man of the pew,
"This is good enough for me."
And he forgets that apart from
the scholars he would have had
no English Bible at all, let alone
a revision of its text; and he
forgets that the readjustment of
views which experts claim he
cannot, in the long run, with-
stand. What the specialists
think to-day he will think to-
morrow, without being able to
help himself. There is no court
of appeal from the consensus of
the scholars. "I am tired of
criticism," quoth he. But criticism will force itself forward
till these questions are dis-

cussed in an equable spirit.
These questions will not be
settled until they are answered.
Nothing is gained by the ostrich
trick of burying the head in
darkness. Everything will be
lost if we put sacred things
under the guardianship of
superstition. Better scepticism
than make-believe. If the Bible
is to retain any authority among
intelligent Englishmen, we must
admit that the antique theories
and traditions which have been
so unquestioningly adopted from
Judaic Pharisees are imperfect;
that errors have been made
about the Bible, and that there
are errors in the Bible in close
combination with highest truth.
Such admissions ought never to
have troubled any one. They
have been, to the disgrace of
the pulpit, a trouble to thousands. It is better that men
should learn the truth from a
believer rather than from an

unbeliever, as they will learn it. It is not fair to your children that you should, for the sake of their faith, keep them in the dark about truths which in after years they are bound to hear, perhaps from men who have no care for their faith.

The Bible is a book of God, but it is not framed after an ideal standard of perfection. That is the great mistake that has been made. The Pope, in a recent encyclical, states that Inspiration is essentially incompatible with error, that it excludes and rejects error. It is sufficient to say that no scholar holds that.

The universe is the work of God, and the students of science once began with their *à priori* theories about that. "The earth," said they, "must be a flat surface; it must be the centre of the universe." And

they "framed eccentrics and epi-
cycles and a wonderful engine
of orbs," and twisted the facts
to correspond. So long as they
held by that fatuous course, the
gates of knowledge were shut
against them.   God did not
make a perfect world such as
they had supposed. His thoughts
are not as our thoughts.

In the same way men said,
"God gave us the Bible, God is
all-wise, therefore the Bible
can hold no mistakes ; it must
be free from all discrepancies,
and its conclusions must agree
with the verified discoveries of
science."   But after a time men
learned that it is not so ; that
science says one thing, the Bible
another.   The man who binds
up the cause of Christianity
with the literal accuracy of the
Bible is no friend of Christianity, for with the rejection
of that theory too often comes
the rejection of the Bible itself,

and faith is shattered. We
have no more reason to expect
Aristotelian logic from the Prophets than Attic Greek from the
Evangelists; but men have
tried to explain, or explain
away, discrepancies and har-
monise impossibilities until
Biblical criticism has become a
by-word for disingenuousness.
Men have applied to the
Bible methods of reconciliation,
which they would be ashamed
to apply to any other book.
They will explain away the dis-
parities in Christ's genealogies,
although from David to Christ
St. Matthew makes twenty-
eight generations, and St. Luke
thirty-eight, with only two
names common to the two
lists.

There is no sign of that
mechanical perfectness which
some presuppose. For instance,
if there is one thing which
we should have imagined as

accurately reported, it is the inscription on Christ's cross. Now, we have four accounts of the Crucifixion, and four inscriptions are repeated : St. Matthew gives " This is Jesus, the King of the Jews"; St. Mark gives " The King of the Jews"; St. Luke gives " This is the King of the Jews"; and St. John gives " Jesus of Nazareth, the King of the Jews." Judge that impartially, and you have fair reliable witness, but a summary end to the notion of infallible witness. There is overwhelming evidence for the authenticity of the New Testament, but the absence of minute accuracy is in itself a hint. It is best to acknowledge such differences as occur quite naturally. Nay, it is the *sine quâ non* of all intellectual honesty in our faith towards the Bible. Let us take the facts ; let the theory take care of itself.

When we first realise the natural way in which the writers of the Bible collected their facts and gave their impressions, we are surprised at the entire absence of claim to supernatural guidance to Divine accuracy. According to the Jewish dictum, "The law speaks with the tongue of the children of men." One of the Evangelists does not profess to be an original narrator, but simply "to set forth in order what witnesses had declared,"—he is an editor who tells us that he has taken due pains to be accurate. Another Evangelist, "who saw, bare record, and his record is true, and he knoweth that he saith true." All the writers have their own characteristics and their favourite forms of expression. St. Paul tells the Corinthians, "I think that I have the Spirit of God," " I have no commandment, but I give my judgment." What could be more cautious and discriminating? How he hesitates in difficult cases! Listen how he corrects himself: "I thank God I baptized none of you save Crispus and Gaius. Yes, beside that I baptized also the household of Stephanus. Beside, I know not whether I baptized any other."

You see that the Bible is not at all what you would have expected a revelation to be,— sixty-six books by different men, variously endowed. It does not consist of golden sayings and rules of life, nor does it give explanations of the philosophical and social problems of the world. It contains history, poetry, drama, memoirs, letters. Great principles are wrapped up in little stories. It tells us how the Israelites tolerated slavery and polygamy; it tells of lust and treachery and crime, for it holds no brief for its own heroes. It is a literature. You cannot pass judgment on a literature in one sentence. And all sorts of moral difficulties arise because the Bible is so different from what we think it ought to be. It is constantly revising and restating itself, because it contains the progress and upward growth of a people. Let the book stand; it does not need our apologies.

What will be the upshot of the present criticism? Is there no peril in reconstruction? Will the veracity of the Bible be impugned or its validity undermined? These are the anxious questions of earnest hearts. Well, reconstruction imperils something; but it must go on nevertheless. What is destroyed is for the most part mere traditional opinion about the Bible—the wood, hay, and

stubble which had been mixed
with what is abiding and
indestructible. Nothing will
be destroyed, unless we choose
to cherish an untenable theory
of Inspiration.

"But is it safe?" asks the
tremulous soul. Oh, ye of little
faith! The universe is so con-
structed by the All-wise God
that nothing but truth is safe.
There is no safety in pusilla-
nimity. The immediate utility
of any truth should not be the
main concern of any honest
man. Do your duty, and trust
to God for the result. Safe! A
ship's true safety is not in lying
water-logged in harbour, but in
voyaging to its far-off port.
Truth is safe anywhere while
God rules. "Give her but
room."

Depend upon it, we may trust
the Bible to do its own work
and make its due impression.
We need not hide the truth

about the Bible in order to get it properly valued. What is Divine in it will speak to men. Try to treat the volume as a flawless chronological or scientific record, and you will be disappointed. Treat it as a means of religious edification, and you cannot fail.

The dominant quality of the Bible is Inspiration; but it is not all inspiring, any more than all the gold region is golden. Or, to use a better simile, the vitalising oxygen is mingled with the nitrogen, and for that very reason is the more serviceable to human life.

The crawling centuries pass, and this book stands forth amid the "literature of power," the classic of the soul; it comes out of a profounder depth of thought than any other book. Oh, the sovereignty of the

Bible does not depend on the
things which critics discuss.
"There is more in the Bible
that finds me," said Coleridge,
"than in all other books put
together." It impresses us with
the idea of God as no other
book does. This age has seen
no more mordant scoffer than
Heine ; but when he lay on the
"mattress grave," from which he
was not to rise again, it was (as
he confesses) the reading of the
Bible which brought him back
to faith and God,—"He that has
lost his God can find Him again
in this book, and towards him
who has never known Him it
wafts the breath of the Divine
Word." "Let mental culture
go on advancing," said Goethe,
"let the natural sciences go on
gaining in breadth and depth,
and the human mind expand
as it may, it will never go
beyond the elevation and moral
culture of Christianity as it

glistens and shines forth in the
Gospel."

We search the world for truth ; we cull
The good, the pure, the beautiful,
From graven stone and written scroll,
From all old flower-fields of the soul ;
And, weary seekers of the best,
We come back laden from the quest,
To find that all the sages said
Is in the book our mothers read.

II.

THE GROWTH OF THE BIBLE.

THE OLD TESTAMENT.

THE GROWTH OF THE BIBLE.

THE OLD TESTAMENT.

"At sundry times and in divers manners."
HEB. i. 1.

MUSSULMANS regard the Koran as a book made in heaven and let down to earth. It is only very ignorant Christians who think the same of the Bible. The very word Scriptures (*scripturæ*) indicates a composite origin; the plural word *Biblia* (the books) was commonly used until the thirteenth century. Among other sacred books of the peoples, the Bible stands like a coralline structure; it is the literature of a race whose genius was for religion, as truly as the genius of Greece was for art, and the genius of Rome for civil organisation. It is a selected national library, in which patriotism and piety are one—a sacred anthology of the Hebrews, miscellaneous in character and form, but carefully chosen to tell the story of a people's gradual approach to a higher ethic and a nobler thought of God, from barbaric beginnings with foul deities and human sacrifices, until it culminates in the teaching of a Father in Heaven Who from His children requires only the self-sacrifice of loving obedience to His Will.

Enquiring into the growth of the Bible, it is necessary to warn you against supposing that the titles of chapters, or the accompanying dates, or the headings of pages have any authority. They are the remains of a system of interpretation adopted by modern theologians, who had arrived at certain dogmatic conclusions, and ingeniously subjected the Bible to the requirements of their theologic system by insinuating these head-lines and guides; they are not integral with the originals and are best disregarded, since they give the impression of an intellectual unity which does not at all exist.

Let me caution you against possible disappointment because of our inability to reach definite and certain conclusions to many of the questions that arise. The argument is complex, and will declare itself only to those who take pains. The masters of criticism differ among themselves. "Dead certainties" belong to an early stage of knowledge and development, and as we grow older we begin to suspect that all is not so sure as we were once apt to believe.

"On all great subjects there is always something more to be said." "Orthodoxy is but the premature conceit of certainty." The novice asks, "If John did not write 'John,' who did? If Moses did not write the Pentateuch, who did?" And in the absence of all definite reply, he assumes airs of triumph. I have stood beside Adam's grave and heard the old question, "Whose grave is it, if it be not Adam's?" That is hardly a conclusive demonstration that the father of our race lies there. And in many questions of Biblical research we must be willing to wait awhile in "adult suspension of judgment," prepared sometimes, like the Patriarch, to go out not knowing whither. Recall those memorable words of Cromwell, "I beseech you, by the mercies of God, remember, it is possible you may be mistaken."

Trying my best to keep abreast of the experts, I can hope only imperfectly to set forth their conclusions ; indeed, the difficulty of the undertaking increases enormously as I make the attempt.

The most casual student of the early books of the Bible must have noticed certain peculiarities in the use of different names for the Divine Being. The first chapter of Genesis always speaks of " God " (Elohim). From the fourth verse of the second chapter to the end of the fourth chapter, we have always the " Lord God." From the fifth chapter to the ninth verse of the sixth chapter, we have always the " Lord " (Jahweh or Jehovah). Now this is not accidental ; and, following the hint given by those facts, a wonderful discovery has been made, for the changing use of the names is accompanied by a marked difference of style in the narration. We are all familiar with the reduplication of the stories in Genesis, which are particularly perplexing since they are not always susceptible of reconciliation. There are two stories of the Creation with striking differences in style and detail; two documents are fused together and lie side by side without an attempt at harmonisation, in such a manner that they could not have been written *currente calamo* by the same author. There are two stories of the Flood: in the former, two of every creature entering the Ark; in the latter, seven pairs of clean animals, two of unclean; and the time of the subsidence of the waters is different. Two stories are artlessly soldered together, but each is homogeneous and consistent in itself. Two ingenuous versions

of the same story continually
occur. Nothing is gained by
straining them into reconciliation. There are two inconsis-
tent accounts of the origin of
" Beersheba," of " Israel," of
" Bethel." There are two in-
congruous lists of the three
wives of Esau. There are two
stories of Abraham's wife being
forcibly attached to a royal
harem, at so late an age that
some commentators suggest a
" preternatural youth." The
stories can, with a little care,
be dissociated. There are two
versions of the Decalogue in
the twentieth and thirty-fourth
chapters of Exodus respectively.
And it is well known that the
reason for the Fourth Commandment in one differs con-
siderably from the reason assigned in the other. Indeed,
the twentieth chapter is ethi-
cally in advance of the thirty-
fourth chapter. How surprised

you would be if, in reading the Ten Commandments, I were to add, "Thou shalt not offer the blood of my sacrifice with leaven," " The firstling of an ass thou shalt redeem with a lamb, and, if thou redeem him not, then shalt thou break his neck." (Exod. xxxiv.) Yet these words were written on the tables. Some of the laws are reiterated, sometimes in the same, sometimes in different language in the Book of Numbers. The period of the service of the Levites is fixed from thirty to fifty years of age, also from twenty-five to fifty years of age, and it was subsequently modified by Ezra to twenty to fifty years of age. In the same book, the rebellion of Korah, Dathan, and Abiram is a confusing amalgam of two distinct incidents. Samuel regarded the people's wish for a king as a sin against God ; yet in Deuteronomy there are provisions for a king.

Now, in view of these anomalies, it may be well for me to give the general theory of the higher critics. The first six books of the Bible—the Hexateuch (Joshua being a close continuation of the first five books)—are anonymous, for there is no ground for the traditional authorship by Moses of books which estimate his character ("Very meek, above all the men who were upon the face of the earth," Numbers xii. 3), and record his death ("No man knoweth of his sepulchre *unto this day*," Deut. xxxiv. 6), and were evidently written by a man who lived on the West of Jordan (Deut. i. 1 and iv. 46), whither Moses never penetrated. Think, also, of the meaning of such verses as Gen. xxxvi. 31, " Before there reigned any king over the children of Israel";

Numbers xv. 32, "While the children of Israel were in the wilderness"; and Gen. xii. 6, "The Canaanite was then in the land." These books have been disentangled or disintegrated into various documents as follows:—First, the Book of the Covenants (Exodus xxi. to xxiii. 19), the oldest part of the Bible, due to Moses, who was the real architect of Israel, binding the people to Jehovah. We know that the "Law of Moses" was originally so brief and simple that it could be written on the stones of an unhewn altar. And it is natural to suppose that whatever the great lawgiver himself actually wrote would be sacredly preserved.

Then come the Elohistic and Jehovistic history books, originating probably in the reign of David or Solomon, with a slightly later document fusing these two. They are the story-book of the Pentateuch, with which we were early familiarised.

Next comes Deuteronomy, a book by itself. Seven hundred years after Moses, you will remember how, under King Josiah, a Book of the Law was found in the temple. It had been so long lost that its provisions were in oblivion, ignored and violated, and the very existence of such a law-book had passed away from memory. It came as an absolute novelty upon the people—like a thunderbolt awakening consternation; it exercised in Judaism an influence as important as Luther's discovery of the Bible in the monastery exercised in Protestantism. It seems impossible to conceive that so precious and sacred a document, the property of the nation, could have been lost. Yet the very

tradition of its existence was
dead, which is as inconceivable
as that besieged citizens should
forget a spring of water.   In
sober fact, the book was written
then, in the interests of ethical
religion.   In their eagerness to
enforce a truth the writers were
led to conceal a fact ; they put
it, as all the Law, under the
authority of Moses, because he
gave the initial impulse to
Israel's national and religious
life, and because they felt that
they were developing his principles.

Next we have the Priestly
Code, which runs from Genesis
to Joshua, and contains nearly
all the sacerdotal regulations of
Exodus, Numbers, and Leviticus, with their historical frame-
work.   This originated in the
captivity, or at least some
little time before it was read
by Ezra and accepted by the
people.   We have all found it

difficult to understand how the prophets could have spoken as they did, if they had known of this priestly code. For instance, Jeremiah (vii. 22) represents God as saying, "For I spake *not* to your fathers nor gave them commandment in the day when I brought them out of Egypt concerning burnt-offerings and sacrifices." And if Isaiah had known of these sacrificial ordinances, how could he have asked, " When ye come to see my face, who hath required this at your hand to tread my courts " ?

Finally, we have the editing of the Hexateuch after the return from the exile ; and for this we are indebted to the Scribes, to whom we also owe the books of Chronicles, Ezra, Nehemiah, and some of the Psalms.

Now, on what main grounds is it supposed that some of the early portions of the Bible had

so late an origin? The question
of Hebrew style cannot be pro-
fitably discussed; but we can
be sure that it is as impossible
for a Hebraist to fail to discriminate between early and
late Hebrew, as it is for us to
confuse the English of Chaucer
with that of Tennyson. Here,
however, is one salient fact
which has contributed to these
striking conclusions: the Law
forbade sacrifice save at a cen-
tral sanctuary, yet all the early
saints and heroes sacrificed
freely—Samuel offering on high
places, Saul building altars,
David and Solomon permit-
ting various local celebrations,
Elijah declaring that the de-
struction of the altars of
Jehovah was a breach of the
Covenant. Yet this was all
wrong according to Deuteronomy. The primitive notion
of sacrifice in all the ancient
world had been a tribal feast

at which the Deity was supposed to partake. Deuteronomy changed all that into a priestly ceremonial, needing for the majority a pilgrimage to Jerusalem. In the earlier Book of the Covenants, every place where God records His name is to be a sanctuary ; the essential feature of Deuteronomy is that there is to be only one altar. After the issue of that book, in other words, after the revolution initiated by Josiah, local places of worship were suppressed. The later prophets were all influenced by that idea, but there is no trace of it in the earlier prophets. Ezekiel, the prophet-priest, who wrote in Babylon, shows the process of transformation out of which issued the complex hierarchical system. There is a free sketch of it in the last nine chapters of his book. where, in imagination, he restores the Temple services.

This is the task that Ezra actually undertook.   It must have occurred to you that all the elaborate hierarchy, with its intricate furniture of ritual, was a late product after many generations ; that it was an impossible creation of a nomad desert tribe.   And, in fact, only late did Jerusalem become the one holy place of the land ; only late came the festivals which imply a settled agricultural life ; only late did the Levitical priesthood become the one sacred order conducting the worship of Jehovah without idolatrous symbolism.

By the captivity Israel was brought into contact with one of the most advanced civilisations of the world, and through it lost its provincialism and race insularity. In the captivity Israel was thrown in upon its inner life, and its religion found its highest reach of thought.

That was the moment of the nation's second birth; "cross fertilisation" of ideas took place, and religion threw off its lingering polytheism. Then came leisure for Israel to look back, and retrospection took form in the new histories of their past. Judges, Samuel, and Kings assumed their present shape. Then came leisure to look within, and new Psalms were written to which adversity lent occasional fierceness, but more frequently a long-drawn sigh to God for relief, or cry of confession and repentance. Then came leisure to look forward, and the national ideal was changed. Instead of a dream of a puissant King, there arose a vision of the righteous, suffering servant of God, and select souls of the nation caught the idea that they were being trained in the school of sorrow, and charged to lead the world into a knowledge of their Eternal Righteous God. In the second part of Isaiah we have the voice of the captivity with all its pathos and passions. The race which had been so unfaithful to its God returned from the Babylonian exile, intent in devotion and fanatical in its excess of zeal for Him. Judaism was born by the Euphrates as Mosaism had been born by the Nile, so it is natural that there should be no hint in the latter constitution, as represented in Leviticus, of the organisation of national life. It is natural that there should be no civil code, so that while whole pages are devoted to costumes and rubrics, we hear nothing of the government of a nation. The idea of a nation is, in fact, supplanted by the idea of a church; the people became a congregation.

Now, all this may be called

destructive criticism, but it is only as a pile of bricks is destroyed when the house is built; instead of unity which was formal and mechanical, the whole becomes vital and organic. The message becomes actualised, and its historic growth is explained; the fascination of the Bible is deepened, while its ethical grandeur is unscathed.

There is an objection which will occur to some minds, and I wish to face it frankly. If our historical sources are so far removed from the events, and not due to contemporaries, how can their testimony be regarded as authoritative? That is a difficulty; but, on the other side, it is also a relief. There are many narratives which are improbable, not to say impossible, of belief. To take one example out of many: In Numbers xxxi. we read that twelve thousand Hebrews slew all the men and married women of Midian, captured thirty-two thousand virgins, and drove off eight hundred thousand head of cattle, all with the Divine sanction. Now, as Dr. Horton says, "There is a type of orthodoxy which deems the Christian faith and hope bound up in the accuracy of that appalling act of barbarity. If this was not commanded by God, there is no word of God spoken to men." Nothing is so detrimental to Christianity as to represent such things as essential. We must long, many of us, for some way of disbelieving that and kindred incidents without throwing aside the truth of the book that contains them, and it is a real relief to find that the name of God may be dissociated from these atrocities. How can we believe that our Heavenly Father ordained (Exod. xxi. 20,

21) that "if a man smite his servant, or his maid, with a rod, and he die under his hand, he shall surely be punished. Notwithstanding, if he continue a day or two, he shall not be punished, for he is his money"? Or (Deut. xiv. 21), "Ye shall not eat of anything that dieth of itself; thou shalt give it to the stranger that is in thy gates, that he may eat it, or thou mayest sell it to an alien"? The characteristic difficulties experienced by most of our fellow-citizens are not speculative and philosophic, but practical and historic difficulties like these. They have keen eyes for the inconsistencies of the Old Testament, and will gladly accept any reasonable method of getting quit of them.

We have in the Bible the long history of a national religious evolution from the time when they deified stones, trees, and

living principles, to the time
when Jehovah was chosen as
the tribal Deity and His worship connected with morality,
and so on to Monotheism,
properly so called. For, remember, the Hebrews were not
pure Monotheists all the while,
but rather, to use the expression
of Max Müller, " Henotheists,"
that is, worshippers of one God
while acknowledging many.
The Decalogue is not strictly
monotheistic, "Thou shalt have
no other gods before Me."
Jehovah is the "Lord of Lords,"
"Who is like unto Thee, Jehovah, among the gods ? " In
Deut. iv. 19, Jehovah is represented as allotting various
nations to various deities, but
retaining Israel for Himself;
and it is continually assumed
that other nations have their
gods, and that banishment
from Canaan is equivalent
to banishment from Jehovah.

You cannot have failed to
have been struck with the continual intrusion of Baal and
the motley divinities of other
lands, and the frequent seduc-
tion of Israel into the vile
licence of their neighbours.
Each house had its teraphim or
domestic divinities, and even
the symbolism of the Temple
was idolatrous (the twelve oxen
holding the laver, the horns of
the altar, the cherubs or cloud
dragons). Indeed, even after
Elijah signally proclaimed the
sole supremacy of Jehovah, the
worship of many gods was
widely retained. Note how in
the twenty-third chapter of the
second Book of Kings, Josiah
" brought forth out of the
Temple of the Lord all the
vessels that were made for Baal
and for Asherah and for the
hosts of heaven . . . put
down the idolatrous priests
whom the kings of Judah had

ordained to burn incense in the high places in the cities of Judah and in the places round about Jerusalem, them also who burned incense unto Baal, to the sun, and to the moon, and to the planets, and to all the hosts of heaven, and he brought out the Asherah from the House of the Lord and turned it into the brook Kidron and stamped it small to powder . . . and he brake down the houses of the Sodomites, that were in the House of the Lord, where the women wove hangings for the Asherah . . . and he defiled Topheth, which is in the valley of the children of Hinnom, that no man might make his son or his daughter to pass through the fire to Molech. And he took away the horses that the kings of Judah had given to the sun, at the entering in of the House of the Lord." And so on throughout the chapter. What the popular religion of Israel continued to be long after this may be inferred from the scornful invective of Jeremiah: "According to the number of thy cities are thy gods, O Judah." The prophetic Religion was far above the level of the masses, and Israel only gradually arrived at the conviction that the sacrifice of righteousness was the only oblation God required. Vestiges of savagery are imbedded in the older books, like "dragons of the slime" in the rocks beneath our feet. But the spiritual genius of Israel sloughed them off and left them behind. It is a great gain to conceive of the Old Testament as representing an evolution from lower to higher things, from the savagery of Deborah's song to the deep inwardness of the penitential Psalms, from a brutal and idolatrous polytheism towards that thought of

God which illumined the mind
of Christ.

Finally, in the gap between
the two Testaments, there was
great activity. They were not
years of decadence and formal-
ism, but most fruitful in religious growth; no prophet arose,
but the sacred books were read
in every synagogue and learnt
in every home. Many sects
sprang into being; in every
village a meeting-house (synagogue) was built, opening its
doors on Sabbath and market
days. Quietly the life deepened
and the nation prepared for its
final development of Religion.

Then in the fulness of time
came the Man. The Law was
the tutor to lead the nation into
the school of Christ, and when
Israel's work was done, the
faithful heart could exclaim,
"Now lettest Thou Thy servant
depart, O Lord, according to
Thy word, in peace; for mine

eyes have seen Thy salvation, which Thou hast prepared before the face of all peoples; a light for revelation to the Gentiles, and the glory of Thy people Israel."

III.

THE GROWTH OF THE BIBLE.

THE NEW TESTAMENT.

THE GROWTH OF THE BIBLE.

THE NEW TESTAMENT.

"Every one therefore which heareth these words of mine, and doeth them, shall be likened unto a wise man, which built his house upon the rock: and the rain descended, and the floods came, and the winds blew, and beat upon that house; and it fell not: for it was founded upon the rock."—ST. MATTHEW vii. 24, 25.

INTEREST is more readily roused in the New Testament than in the Old, for it is the historic source of our faith, the well-spring of all that is best in Christendom. These short records have done more to regenerate mankind than all the writings of philosophers and moralists; they made the death of Christ into the birth of Christendom.

It is impossible for me now to discuss the formation of the Canon—that were too long a story : how in the early centuries there grew up around the young Religion an enormous mass of Christian literature, much of it apocalyptic, more of it spurious, most of it valueless ; how about a hundred years after Christ men began to make different selections of this literature according to their predilections ; how in an age of credulity, in which the science of criticism did not so much as exist, some books oscillated long between acceptance and rejection ; how, largely under the influence of Augustine, at the end of the fourth century, a final selection was made and the Canon closed, the guiding principle of choice being pious feeling and apos-

tolic sanction. But the mere
sketch of the story is sufficient
to assure us that the New Testament in its integrity is not a
miraculous whole.

There are many hundreds of
versions of the text ; the oldest
manuscripts (Sinaitic and Vati-
can) date from the fourth century, while the oldest Hebrew
manuscripts of the Old Testament are not older than the
tenth century, though there are
earlier copies of the Greek
Septuagint Version (200 B.C.).
It is a noteworthy fact that the
older the manuscripts are, the
more they vary among themselves, for the more free and
unconstrained their writers
were about modifying the record. The order of the books in
our New Testament is due, not
to chronological sequence, but
broadly to their subject-matter,
as was the case with the arrangement of the Old Testament.

5

There is no reason to suppose
that the original writers were
the amanuenses of God, super-
naturally guarded from inac-
curacy.   The glory of their
Master has irradiated them; but,
in truth, they were very simple
men unused to literary labour.
And it is good for the world
that it was so, for Christ needed
no record save the simplest.
Literary genius on the part of
His biographers would have
obscured more than it revealed.
The Evangelists were men who
could not have invented the
great words and deeds which
they reported ; and all the in-
firmities of their memory and
imperfections of their style
could not mar the picture which
they drew of the " sinless years
that breathed the Syrian blue."

Jesus Himself wrote nothing ;
He did not write the truth, He
was the Truth.   He gave His
disciples no command to pub-

lish, but to preach. His epistles
were to be the regenerate lives
of His apostles. His testament
was to be written in the incar-
nate living words of such as
were being saved by Him. No
daily record of Christ's life had
been kept. There was no Bos-
well among the Twelve. And
when Jesus had gone from them
the disciples believed that He
would speedily return. That
illusion suffused their whole
nature. No conviction was
more strong or influential.
What need, then, of writing
books about Him when He
would be here so soon ? Indeed,
the committing of a record to
writing for the sake of posterity
would undoubtedly seem to
many of them to imply a lack
of faith in His promise. They
did not at first realise the world-
wide mission of their Lord, still
less did they guess the thousands of years which must

elapse before His kingdom should be won. It does not come natural to peasants to write books, and nothing was farther from the intentions of those Galileans. Only the pressure of circumstances forced the New Testament from the narrow and comparatively un-cultured circles of the primitive churches.

They preached Christ, and their sermons were largely com-posed of summaries of His life. These summaries settled into definite "forms of teaching" or traditions, of which we have examples in St. Paul's accounts of the Lord's Supper and the Resurrection (1 Cor. xi. 23-25, xv. 3-8). But as the generation of men who had seen the Lord passed away, younger Christians desired to have in some written form the testimony associated with the names of the elders. Thus it was that the first

informal memoirs of the Great
Life came to be written—not
treatises, but memorabilia.
Many, doubtless, had gradually
made private memoranda for
their own use, without a
thought of collecting or editing them for the general body
of Christians; still less with
any idea of writing for the
information of those without; and still less, again, with
any purpose of shaping books
that would endure till the end
of the world. So it came to pass
that the first Christian Scriptures were not highly regarded;
for men did not (Papias A.D.
140) "consider things taken
from books to be of such good
to them as things from the
living, abiding voice." But the
Master's words were very precious, and many reminiscences
gathered round them as they
wrote. We have traces of Gospels written by Peter, Thomas,

Bartholomew, and others. For many, like St. Luke, " took in hand to set forth in order a declaration of those things which are surely believed among us," and they depended for their authorities on the common stock of Christian memory.

We have four Gospels, or, as I should prefer to say, four records of the Gospel, for, according to New Testament usage, " Gospel" never denoted a written word; it stood for the substance of the message of Christ. Our books are, in each case, the Gospel " *according to* " such an one ; not as claiming his actual authorship, but as implying the agreement of their contents with the recognised document or tradition coming from that original. Three of these little books are of quite different character from the fourth, and they are classed

together as the Synoptics,
because they give the same
synopsis of events, agree in
general plan, for the most part
in the narratives, and sometimes in the very words. Yet
though they are so intimately
connected, they are quite independent. They were not written
in collusion, for each has its in-
dividual character and had its
own editor. Indeed, one of the
great gains of modern criticism
is the universal admission of
the specialists that the Evangelists meant in good faith to
write history. Of late the
general confidence in the Scripture writers has much increased.
They were entirely set on accuracy so far as that was possible to them.

Our Book of St. Mark is the
shortest and the earliest of the
four; it is a clear, straight-
forward, matter-of-fact narrative. You can read it at a

sitting, and it produces the impression of being a faithful story. We have it in its primitive condition, or nearly so, as it left the hand of St. Mark, who derived his information mainly from St. Peter, and wrote probably in Rome about the year 70. It is well understood that St. Matthew made a collection of the sayings of Jesus in the Aramaic language, in which He spoke. This is not extant, but it was largely used in combination with the record of St. Mark to furnish the material of our Books of St. Matthew and St. Luke, St. Matthew drawing more freely on the collection of sayings, St. Luke more freely on the Book of St. Mark. So that we have the definite authority of one Apostle, St. Matthew, for the sayings; and, on the other hand, for the acts of Jesus, we have the authority of another Apostle,

St. Peter, of whose preaching the Book of St. Mark is the digest.

Our Book of St. Matthew was written for Jews. It aims to show that Jesus was the Messiah, foretold for Israel, and that His Gospel had its root in Judaism. It is full of references to the Old Testament, and Christ's lineage is traced to Abraham, the father of all Hebrews. It emphasizes the conservative position of our Lord towards the Law, and dwells on His faithful adherence to Jewish customs. Its key-note may be said to be, "Think not that I am come to destroy the law or the prophets; I am not come to destroy, but to fulfil." (Compare the remarkable passage in which Jesus is represented as acquiescing in Rabbinical authority and tradition, xxiii. 2, 3.)

Our Book of St. Luke was

probably written originally by
the Gentile physician who was
the companion of St. Paul. Its
sympathies are more catholic
than those of St. Matthew, and
it was intended for a wider
circle. The genealogy of Jesus
is traced past Abraham to
Adam, for he is more than the
Messiah of Israel; He is the Son
of Man who is to lighten the
Gentiles with the Gospel of
peace and goodwill to all.
According to St. Luke, the first
sermon of Jesus was founded
on that part of Isaiah which
most finely transcends the
bounds of Jewry. St. Luke
alone gives the stories of the
Good Samaritan, the Pharisee
and Publican, and the Prodigal
Son; St. Luke emphasizes
Jesus' friendship for publicans
and sinners; St. Luke accentuates His broad human tolerance
and His tenderness to the poor.
Renan calls it the most beauti-

ful book ever written; and
many of you will remember
its impression made on the
Greek girl in Cardinal New-
man's "Callista." From St.
Luke's preface we learn with
what pains he made his com-
pilation. Without claiming
chronological accuracy, he
insists that he is bearing reliable witness, and acknowledges
his obligations to those who
"from the beginning were eye-
witnesses and ministers of the
Word." Among other sources
before him as he wrote was
our Book of St. Mark, which he
must have regarded as a reliable report, for he made it the
frame within which he worked
up additional material.

There is only one other point
that I feel obliged to add in regard to the Synoptics. Our Books
of St. Matthew and St. Luke add
independent accounts of Jesus'
birth and infancy, for which

there is no parallel in the older
Book of St. Mark, which lays
the "Beginning of the Gospel"
and Christ's story in the preaching of St. John the Baptist.
Those lovely nativity stories,
which have seized on the imagination and nestle in the heart
of Christendom, cannot, therefore, be fairly regarded as of the
same compelling authority as
the rest of the narrative which
is common to the three Books.
But, be it remembered, they are
not so important either. Jesus
Himself never referred to them,
and argued (Matt. xxii. 41-45)
against the necessity of a
Davidic descent. The fourth
Gospel does not found its claim
for Christ as the Eternal Word
on a miraculous conception,
which is the more strange, if
its author was actually the be-
loved disciple to whose care
Jesus committed His mother.
St. Paul does not seem con-

scious of such an idea, for he
does not make a solitary refer-
ence to the stories in question,
nor do the other books of the
New Testament give the most
shadowed hint of them. We
may reassure ourselves that
the Divinity of Christ does
not rest on them. They were
accepted by the Early Church
as a fulfilment of an Old Testament oracle (Isaiah vii. 14),
and, in view of the doctrine
of Original Sin, as a consistent account of the birth of
the Holy One who knew no
sin ; they were to them the
only adequate explanation. But
that explanation was not regarded as an essential element
of faith in Him, and it is well
to reduce it to its proper dimen-
sions, and to realise that the
sinlessness of Christ is His real
Divinity, and constitutes Him
the world's Saviour from sin.

The problem of the Gospel

according to St. John is very
difficult, but extremely interesting in all its phases.   Some
experts are confident beyond all
doubt that the Apostle John
wrote it; some equally learned
are equally confident that he is
the last person in Christendom
who could have written it.   It
seems to me that in this vexed
question most men tend to a
judgment in accord with their
personal and religious idiosyn-
crasies, and (though you may
catch the note of personal prejudice in this thought) that
recent research and criticism
are making it practically certain
that the fourth Gospel was the
work either of John or of a disciple under his inspiring influence.   The book differs essentially from the Synoptics; it is
more obviously an organic
whole than they.   It contains
very little of the common
tradition that underlies them;

for example, though, according to St. Matthew, Jesus never spoke without a parable, St. John does not relate a single parable, nor does the very word occur. The book introduces new material, and uses all in quite a new style and spirit, betokening the personal authorship of a man of original mind, mystic temper, and strong spiritual individuality. It is extremely instructive to observe that the writer introduces the entirely original conferences of our Lord with Nicodemus, with the woman of Samaria, and with the Greeks who desired to see Him; but in each case the character who is introduced to start the discourse of Jesus is allowed forthwith to drop out of sight, showing that didactic considerations determine the writer, his predominant interest being in the religious import of the stories

he tells. His animating motive
is to convince his readers that
Jesus is the Son of God. It
appears to me that the aged
disciple, recalling the dear past,
saw it all transfigured in the
light of his long spiritual ex-
perience and under the influence of his later Greek ideal-
ism. He presupposes that his
readers are already familiar
with the main facts. His function is not to tell the story of
Jesus, but to interpret it, as a
poet, with " sovereign hand-
ling," less concerned with incidents than with their inner
meaning. Sometimes it is impossible to say where Christ's
addresses begin or end, so freely
does the writer treat his subject-
matter; as though it were quite
unnecessary to distinguish between what the Lord said and
what grew out of it. The ideas
are Christ's, the interpretation
is the writer's. St. John is de-

termined to set forth the glory
he had seen in the Word made
flesh, the utterance of God's
love, the embodiment of human
perfection and Divine excel-
lence, the Light of the world,
the Bread of Life, the Shepherd,
the Way, the Truth, the Life.
He does not so much endeavour
to present Christ as the Logos,
as to show that the truths
contained in that familiar doctrine are better expressed in
Him their true Representa-
tion.

> Lo, He comes,
> Hungry, thirsty, homeless, cold;
> Hungry, by whom saints are fed
> With the eternal living bread;
> Thirsty, from whose pierced side
> Living waters spring and glide;
> Cold and bare He comes, who never
> Can put off His robe of light;
> Homeless, who must dwell for ever
> In the Father's bosom bright.

That is the aim of the fourth
Gospel; and, in attaining that

aim, it becomes the supreme
book of the New Testament,
"the heart of Christ," " the echo
of the older Gospels in the upper
choir."

The "Acts of the Apostles"
was written by one who was
witness of the later part of the
incidents he reports.   It is a
summary of the history of the
Early Church, as the Early
Church conceived its own nativity ; though it is impossible
for us to believe with the same
assurance as they, that Philip
was transported through the
air (chapter viii. 39), or that
Paul's handkerchief healed the
sick (xix. 12). A comparison
of the book with particulars in-
cidentally detailed in St. Paul's
Epistles is very instructive.

The library of books which
we assuredly owe to St. Paul
has been steadily growing of
late. A short time ago, and
only four Epistles were unani-

mously assigned to him—
Romans, Galatians, and the
first and second of Corinthians;
they were frequently called the
"great quadrilateral of Christianity." Now, the first of
Thessalonians is regarded as
authentic, the earliest of his
letters and probably the oldest
book of the New Testament,
being written in A.D. 52 in
order to give the Thessalonians
better instructions concerning
Christ's return. St. Paul believed the Parousia would occur
in his own lifetime (iv. 15-17),
but he wrote to calm their
expectations and exhort them
to quiet industry as the
best preparation. The second
Epistle to the same Church may
not be in its original form, but
it also calls to order the idle
and disorderly. The Epistles to
the Philippians, Colossians, and
Ephesians are now accepted by
the majority of critics. But the

pastoral Epistles are much more doubtful, both by reason of their contents and the peculiarities of their style.

We cannot exaggerate our indebtedness to the great Apostle, who had higher intellectual understanding of our Lord's teaching than had any around him. But it is well to remember that he did not issue his opinions as though they were Papal Bulls, but frequently used such phrases of modesty and self-restraint as " I speak as a man," " I speak not after the Lord but as in foolishness." So that it is not prudent to take all his opinions as oracles; for example, his suggestion to Timothy (if it was his), that he should use " a little wine," is not to be taken as a general edict for all time; nor his prejudice against feminine oratory, as if women, however capable, were perpetually bound, on that account, to retain their seats in silence; nor his low opinion of marriage as the Christian ideal. Still less wise is it to quote an isolated, splintered fragment of his writing as an axiom from which to deduce a system of theology or ecclesiasticism; though such is a form of misquotation to which St. Paul has from of old been peculiarly liable (2 Peter iii. 16). Sacred and useful as are these Epistles, we must go back to the Gospels to find the simplicity that was in Christ. And even

They are but broken lights of Thee,
And Thou, O Lord, art more than they.

As to the other Epistles: That to the Hebrews may have been written by Apollos or by Barnabas, amid the disappearance of the Temple and the old Jewish cultus, the author seeking to show the relation of the old

Covenant to the new order introduced by Christ. With that end in view the Old Testament is treated homiletically in that profoundly religious Epistle, which we owe to an unknown hand.

The Epistle of James does not claim to be written by an Apostle. It is an elementary ethical letter addressed to Jews abroad, saying little about Christ, and quoting much practical counsel from the Books of Wisdom and Ecclesiasticus. If in some respects his teaching is difficult to reconcile with that of St. Paul, I remind you that the echo of Divine truth in different souls is very varied. " When God makes a prophet He does not unmake the man."

The Epistles of St. Peter are very disappointing. Whether the first be genuine or not, it is certainly unimportant. The second is credited by none,

being a work compiled from the
Epistle of Jude. This last is a
companion letter to that of
James, the author's brother.
He makes quotations from the
Books of Enoch and the As-
sumption of Moses.

The first Epistle of St. John
is simple and evangelic; it has
all the character of the fourth
Gospel, and was probably
written by the same hand.
The second and third Epistles
of St. John are only echoes of
the first, were only late recognised as Canonical, and contain
no new truth. The Book of
Revelation belongs to the very
large class of literature issued
when calamities and persecu-
tions broke on the Church. It
is the work of "John the Theo-
logian," bidding men be of good
courage, since the Lord will
quickly come to save His own,
and the celestial Jerusalem
shall arise instead of the ruined

capital which Rome had devastated. The basis of the book is a purely Jewish document revised by one whose conception of the true Israel is the countless multitude bought with the blood of the Lamb. We may not see much practical worth in this or some other of the books, but it does not become us to treat lightly words which have stood the accumulated judgment of centuries. Depend upon it, a correct canon of judgment for us is that they are valuable in proportion as they are in touch with the Spirit of Christ.

Finally, let us never forget that it is the worth of Christ that substantiates and validates the New Testament. Its supreme value is in its presentation of that blessed and selfless life, which has so slowly risen on the world in its true beauty. He holds Christendom

about Him as the sun draws
the planets. "The Greatest of
the Great," He is more rever-
ently loved than all other,
transcendently above us, yet so
real that we find in Him our
brother and friend. Goethe,
the great apostle of culture,
advised his readers that they
should every day read a fine
thought, look at a beautiful
picture, and hear lovely music.
For the sake of Christian
culture nothing is better than
that every day we should stand
for a moment beside Christ,
listen to a word of His, and get
into sympathetic contact with
His mind. And that, not to
increase æsthetic admiration,
but to deepen our saving knowledge of Him, who strengthens
us in good and warms the heart
with holy love. For such a
daily exercise of devotion and
religious energy we may recall
Christ's own promise: "Every

one therefore which heareth these words of Mine, and doeth them, shall be likened unto a wise man, which built his house upon the rock: and the rain descended, and the floods came, and the winds blew, and beat upon that house; and it fell not: for it was founded upon the rock."

IV.

MISLEADING THEORIES

MISLEADING THEORIES.

" If thou take forth the precious from the vile, thou shalt be as My mouth, saith the Lord."—JER. xv. 19, 20.

LET me remind you that while some time must elapse before the results of historical criticism are absorbed, we have already the immediate advantage of being delivered from the misleading theories of the Bible which have wrought so much mischief. To the allegation that has been made, "Such sermons are unsettling," I reply plainly that most of the infidelity in Christendom has been produced by the untenable dictum that the Bible is the flawless autograph of God. Voltaire was trained by

the Jesuits, Renan was educated
in the intensely orthodox semi-
nary of St. Sulpice, Bradlaugh
was reared in narrow Evan-
gelicalism, George Eliot's Posi-
tivism was the reaction from
impossible doctrines instilled
in early days; and most intellectual men who reject
the Bible and break away
from "the Christ our Human
Brother and Friend," owe their
loss to the fact that they were
taught to build their religion
upon the Bible instead of treat-
ing the Bible as the outcome of
religion.

The doctrine of infallibility
is due to the craving for an
authoritative external proof of
religious belief. The infallibility of the Bible is a figment
of the intellect precisely on a
par with the infallibility of the
Pope. Men want to be rid of
the long struggle after truth,
so they invest either an indi-

vidual or a book with the requisite authority. All that a man has will he give for certainty. It is a dream ; for they forget that the postulate of infallibility in priest or Bible is practically void, apart from a prior infallibility in self.

Suppose the Bible be infallible, still the text is susceptible of many interpretations. One finds written there the necessity of immersion ; another, sacramental grace ; another, apostolic succession, non-resistance, and the rest. An infallible book is useless apart from an infallible interpretation.

Suppose the Bible be infallible, what is included in the Bible ? The All-wise has not given clear definition as to what constitutes the Bible. The history of the formation of the Canon is most disappointing from that aspect. It was based broadly on the survival of the

fittest, according to the judgment of the leading churchmen
of the day. The men who
framed it could not get beyond
possibilities; and it is still prob-
lematic whether it would have
not been better had they included such books as Ecclesiasticus and Wisdom, and excluded
books of such slight literary
merit and spiritual significance
as Esther and the Chronicles.
You are aware that the Roman
Church includes the Apocrypha
within the Canon, as it is
included in the volume that
has always lain in this pulpit.

But taking the Canon as we
usually understand it, we do not
find any writer claiming that
he worked under the direction
of irresistible power, nor does
the Bible in any place treat
itself as a body of infallible
oracles. I desire to emphasize
this, because the objections
to Biblical infallibility cannot

possibly touch the authority of the Bible, unless the Bible itself profess to be infallible. Clearly the New Testament writers did not regard the Old Testament as infallible, or they would not have quoted it as they did, without care for verbal accuracy, continually accommodating its word to another purpose than that which was originally intended (Matt. ii. 15, 18; xxvii. 9, 10; Romans i. 17; 1 Peter ii. 6). Nor did Christ countenance any such theory of the Old Testament. He treated it with loving reverence, and studied it with care; but He bespoke absolute freedom from the bondage of the letter. Nor did the apostles say, "Believe the Bible or perish," but "Believe Christ and be saved." They would have had small sympathy with the theory that finds spiritual resting ground on things, instead of in the Living God.

Think of it, and you will see that a revelation perfect with heavenly excellences and powers would have been to man an undecipherable language. There is no sign that God ever gave an infallible guide at all, nor that He could ever educate man in that way. In the Old Testament He expected Israel to recognise His message by the truth that was in it. No miraculous help was vouchsafed for its recognition, nor could it have been usefully bestowed. They were to know the truth by the way in which it searched their hearts and consciences. How else can truth be known? How can the false prophet be distinguished from the true, save by the power of his message? How can anything external authenticate a spiritual truth? What relation is there between physical power and spiritual truth ? Its appreciation depends on sympathy; spiritual things are spiritually discerned. But, indeed, to speak plainly, the Bible is not a *vade mecum* to furnish rules of action when you are perplexed with difficulties; its *aim* is not to settle debate, but to train men to govern and guide themselves. It is not a directory, but an inspiration to us that we may fight against sin and all the misery that sin begets. Its great purpose is not to lay on us a Divine " *Thou shalt,*" but to kindle in us a Divine " *I ought.*" And it is not so much guidance that we need as something far more searching and kindling; not substitutes for thought, but stimulus to thinking. The Bible does not reveal truths inaccessible to reason, but "transmutes the probabilities of reason into the verities of faith." We have to read as wise men, and judge what the Spirit saith to the Churches. If the purpose of the Bible be to compose all our differences, and settle us all in intellectual union, the Bible has manifestly failed of its purpose. Its aim is, in truth, dynamic ; it belongs to the " literature of power."

Now, on the theory of an infallible book, all its contents are raised, or reduced, to one level. The reasoning is cogent enough :—" The Bible is God's Word ; God's Word is absolutely true ; therefore all Scripture is equally authoritative and infallible." So the Bible becomes a kind of fourth Person of the Blessed Trinity. And we are landed in endless contradictions, for what St. Paul declared " weak and beggarly elements " are as Divine as his own Psalm of Charity ; and the words of our Master are neutralised by being tied to dead traditions. There is only one choice — all or none. " Thus saith the Lord " is behind all.

It is a desperate and fatuous alternative. We know that the Jews extracted texts from their Scriptures, and made talismanic charms of them, nailed them on doors, wrote them on walls, bound them round their brows. It was not more superstitious or idolatrous than is the determination to find the Word of God in everything included in the Bible. So slave-holders found proof texts for their brutalities, and Mormons for their license. So for many centuries men read, " Thou shalt not suffer a witch to live," and thousands of poor wretches were murdered in the Name of God. (Even Luther said, " I would have no compassion on witches; I would burn them all.")

Treat the Bible as a homo-

geneous whole; and the stories
of Olympian vengeance and
miraculous injustice, the de-
struction of Sennacherib's army
and the Psalms of inhuman
imprecation, legal technical-
ities and Levitical trivialities,
are as Divine as the fifty-third
chapter of Isaiah or the four-
teenth chapter of St. John.
There are no degrees of comparison in infallibility.

It will be superfluous for most
of you that I should labour this
point. But suppose an intelligent lad learns that Almighty
God ordered a massacre of
harmless people, as atrocious
as that of the Armenians by
the Turks; that He struck a
man dead for preventing the
Ark from falling from a cart;
that He sent a plague on a
capital city because a king took
a census of the population.
And he is told "It is wicked to
doubt these things." Is not his

sense of right and wrong perplexed? Is it not best to say frankly, "My boy, they pitiably misunderstood God, they thought He was altogether like themselves"? We cannot be sure that our highest thoughts concerning God are necessarily true, but we can be sure that all thoughts about God, below our highest, are necessarily false. And, in the light of that conviction, we are compelled to discriminate between various parts of the Scriptures. Treat all the Scriptures as equally fertile soil, and men will end by regarding it as all equally desert. "Take forth the precious from the vile."

The whole form and fashion of the volume is against this rigorous theory. The Bible is constantly revising itself and improving itself; old things pass away, and better things succeed. How should this book

of survivals from over so long
a period be of like nature and
authority throughout ? It is
the long history of the idea of
the redemptive action of God ; it
is the spiritual autobiography
of a people from its childhood
to its maturity ; it consists of
the most miscellaneous collection — legend, history, and
family genealogy, ecclesiastical
ritual and rubric, proverbs and
folk-lore, battle songs and love
songs, dramas and novelettes,
memoirs, doctrinal treatises and
friendly letters—many of them
anonymous, many pseudony-
mous. Let the Bible speak for
itself. Why should we make it
speak as the Scribes ? They
began by claiming authority
and, on that ground, acceptance.
Let the Bible speak for itself.
The less we ask of its readers
beforehand, the better. To impose conditions is a gratuitous
and noxious trial of faith.

Don't protect it by a dogma of infallibility, or you discredit it. As well shore up Helvellyn with a few beams. The Bible stood well enough in its own strength before that crude defence was reared around it, and it will stand long after that crudity is forgotten. Reverence for the Bible thrives better in the light of history and fact than in the mystic darkness of supernaturalism.

When, as a young man, I found evidences of legendary detritus in the Bible, ought I to have thrown the book away and given up the idea of becoming a minister ? Of course I was forbidden by conscience to enter a church where freedom would be denied, but I was at liberty to seek an honest position among Independents, to whom catholicism and progressivism are second nature. I do not consider that I am bound, as minister of Christ, to defend Abram's cruel treatment of Hagar, the duplicity of Jacob, or the treachery of Jael; it is not my duty to apologise for the sins of the "Man after God's own heart"; I do not hold a brief for Elisha who called out bears to devour the children who gave him a nickname; I have nothing to say in favour of the making of a woman from a man's rib, or the abnormally low specific gravity of iron axes, or the temporary stoppage of the sun in the heavens, or any other miracles to which neither my intellect nor my conscience responds. Neither you nor I are bound to acquiesce in all the sentiments of Ecclesiastes, or to believe Micaiah when he said, "The Lord sent a lying spirit." What do we lose by relegating to legendary folk-lore Samson's slaying of thousands with the jaw of an ass.

or his tying brands to the tails of three hundred foxes? Such things *elsewhere* would cause no difficulty; let us apply ordinary standards of judgment. When you read a book you find no difficulty in determining what deserves your admiration or in judging what is debasing and poor; you trust your own sagacity. What your heart proves good to you, alone is good to you. No number of " Thus saith the Lords " can induce or help us to square the Eden story with archæology, Babel with ethnology, Jonah with ichthyology, or the one-windowed ark, crowded with sets of all the living creatures of the world, with zoology. Reverence should make us pause before we call this the Word of God. " Where the human mind is concerned, it is idle to speak of an authority which can simply be imposed. There neither is nor can be such a thing. The real question is whether there is an authority which can impose itself, which can freely win the recognition and surrender of the mind and heart of man."

Many sincere men have been staggered by these things; but when their intellect or their better nature rebelled, they felt guilty of arraigning God. "Thus saith the Lord," said the Hebrews. And we have to occidentalise the phrase before we see that it was but the voice of the Hebrew conscience in various stages of advance. It is a relief to be able to recognise that, to find oneself possessed of a serene faith which no such words can affect, nor the removal of such words disturb.

Again, on the theory of infallibility, the Bible becomes a finality all round, so that inquiry and investigation thereafter are an impertinence. Research is barred, as by a statute-book, to human thought; we are anchored here. I believe with all my heart that we have a final revelation of God's loving and redeeming purpose in Christ, so that no improvement therein is possible or conceivable; but in all other respects the Bible is not a final authority, and all attempts, for instance, to make the science of the Bible tally with modern science is labour thrown away through a gigantic misconception. In the first chapter of Genesis Creation is portrayed in six stages. The order does not correspond with the actual course of events as stamped on the record of the rocks in tables of stone. There are many "harmonies," but it is very difficult to reconcile the harmonies. The whole passage is not a treatise of science, but

a devotional poem of Creation.
The writer swept in masterly
survey over all created things,
collected them into six congruous groups, and declared
each group the work of Almighty God. It is not geology;
it is theology. The truths that
are too vast for our human
grasp are seen in this spiritual
Song of Creation, casting their
shadow on the early imagination of the race—God, behind
all appearances, the Creator.

There is not in all the Bible
a final utterance on science.
Catholics complain that we
Protestants will not believe in
the progressive illumination of
the Christian Church; that we
leave no room for continuous
revelation of the mind of God.
I fear that we do injustice to
Rome in harping so much on her
fear of the Bible, which fear has
been largely the result of reaction against Protestant idola-

try of the Bible. In the middle ages (as Mr. Baldwin Brown pointed out in the most memorable of all his books, " First Principles of Ecclesiastical Truth"), Rome frequently translated the Bible into the vernacular, and always based her theology on Scripture as the ultimate authority. The New Testament of Erasmus with its caustic comments went through its many editions with the approbation of Pope Leo X. The difference between Rome and the Reformers lay in this—that Rome regarded the Bible as full of infallible truths about doctrines and morals, and held that saving faith is in assent thereto, according to the finding of Mother Church. Rome would convert the Bible into a sacerdotal trust. Luther, Calvin, and Zwingle found in the Bible personal fellowship with the Redeeming God, and taught

that the chief end of the
Bible is to bring God nearer
that we may trust Him. That
is the Protestant doctrine,
which I unfeignedly hold, and
to which I always give earnest
utterance. But it seems to me
that many Evangelicals who
abhor Popery really hold the
mediæval rather than the Re-
formation idea of Scripture.
They have transferred the interest from the Word of God to
the record of the Word, and
invested that record with attri-
butes which cannot belong to
it. There cannot be finality in
the revelation of the Infinite,
whose Spirit evermore guides
us into all truth.

Lastly, the theory of infallibility makes the Bible a mechanical puzzle. The most
wonderful interpretations find
some justification for themselves; the most egregious
folly of piety has something

to plead. The doctrine of the Trinity, that "crowning gift of the Spirit to the Church through the resourcefulness of Greek intellect," has been found in the plural noun which is used in Genesis for the Divine Being. The doctrine of the Atonement is discerned in the scapegoat of Azazel, and Rahab's red cord from the window is typical of Christ's Blood. The total depravity of man is in the wails of Jeremiah, and ecclesiastical allegories are entwined in the Song of Solomon. The main results of modern science are anticipated in cryptograms, which also indicate the course of European history. Scripture is turned into Sibylline leaves and consulted about the fall of the Papacy, the return of the Jews to Palestine, the approach of the end of the ages—about anything, in short, rather than about the

Divine Humanity to which they point. Nor is the grave folly of these grotesque perversions confined to the ignorant classes. Here is an interpretation by Swedenborg :— " And Rebecca arose (hereby is signified the elevation of the affection of truth), and her damsels (hereby are signified the subservient affections), and they rode upon camels (hereby is signified the intellectual principle elevated above natural scientifics)."

In this lamentable way the Bible becomes the dead prey of the dogmatists, and on this style anything may be made to mean anything else. Language has a legitimate meaning; we want to know not what Scripture may be made to mean, but what it does mean. It is difficult enough already to ascertain the precise meaning of some passages, but it would be impossible if every passage might have many interpretations.

That is the outcome of the prevalence of the theory of infallibility. I have shown that the Bible makes no such claim for itself. Dean Stanley expressed the wish that he might awhile be Pope, and regarded as infallible; for in virtue of his infallibility he would straightway decree that he was fallible. Now in regard to the claim that is made, not by but for the Bible, there remains to me the ungracious task of showing how impossible a claim it is. I would not speak thus did I not believe that Bibliolatry is a most mischievous superstition, and did we not all know that some advocates of Christ stake the whole credit of His religion on the absence of mistakes within the sacred Canon. These good men do not realise the harm they do to the cause they love, nor how thorny is the crown they thrust on the Bible. Some of you doubtless feel as if I were, in these sermons, breaking the staff of your life ; but I ask you to suspend judgment till I arrive at the end. I am negative only in the interests of something better. Every departure from popular belief seems at first destructive: it needs keen eyes to perceive the germ of the bud which is to replace the fallen leaf. I believe that criticism makes the Bible more real, more precious, and more useful ; that the whole book becomes more easy of apprehension, and is reduced from confusion to order. While to my own mind there is no practical importance in discussing errors of the Bible, I am bound with wholesome brevity to show, ere I finally dismiss the subject, the utter impracticability of the high and dry

theory of inerrancy. Many of
you well know the examples ;
but inasmuch as a certain
devout inattention is thought
to be the appropriate medium
for the discernment of Biblical
truth, some of you may not
have noticed them.

II. Samuel xxiv. 1 : God moved
David to number the people,
and there were found in Israel
eight hundred thousand warriors, in Judah five hundred
thousand warriors. I. Chron.
xxi. 1 : Satan moved David to
number the people, and there
were found in Israel one million
one hundred thousand warriors,
and in Judah four hundred
and seventy thousand, without
counting Levi and Benjamin.
" When God writes history He
will be at least as accurate as
Bishop Stubbs or Mr. Gardiner."

II. Samuel xxiv. 24: David
paid to Araunah for his thresh-
ing floor fifty shekels of silver,

but in I. Chron. xxi. 25, six hundred shekels of gold.

II. Chron. xiv. 1, xv. 19: Asa reigned peacefully, "The land was quiet ten years . . . to the thirty-fifth year of his reign there was no war." But I. Kings xv. 16, "there was war between Asa and Baasha all their days." The very conservative Professor Sayce remarks that "Assyrian inscriptions have shown that the chronology of the Book of Kings is hopelessly wrong."

Matthew xxvii. 9 quotes as from Jeremiah what you find in Zechariah. The obvious slip of memory in no way invalidates his trustworthiness as a narrator. Calvin confessed the discrepancy and contemptuously dismissed it as unimportant.

Stephen, "a man full of faith and of the Holy Ghost . . . full of grace and power," said (Acts vii. 16) that Abram bought the sepulchre in Shechem of the

sons of Hamor, but Genesis xxiii.
16, 17, declares the purchase of
Machpelah made of Ephron the
Hittite, and Genesis xxxiii. 19,
says that Jacob bought the
ground in Shechem of the sons
of Hamor. Calvin candidly
confessed, " Stephen evidently
made a mistake." Of course he
confounded two transactions.

These are not " inventions of
the enemy " ; they are straight-
forward quotations. Now, in
the presence of errors such as
these, which no man who is at
the same time honest and intelligent can possibly deny, who
are the true friends of the
Bible ? They who admit that
there are errors, and affirm that
the worth of the Bible lies in
quite another sphere than
exactitude of information ; or
they who deny, in the face of
palpable evidence, that there
are any errors, and protest
that if there were but one,

the cause of the Bible would be ruined ? Or, to put it in another way, is it right to stake such a momentous result on such a paltry issue ? An issue, remember, which ought never to have been raised at all, and one to which there is but one possible ending—infidelity. The Bible is wounded in the house of its friends. There is just one way of retreat ; one may say, "The original manuscripts were free from error." The assumption is, of course, baseless. It is worse than ludicrous to suppose that Providence worked an initial miracle, which, for all practical purposes, might as well never have been wrought. Whatever we think, let us be free from disingenuousness.

I have confessed plainly there are mistakes. However you may wish to hold the contrary opinion, there is, I think, no opportunity for you to do so, for no man has a right to believe anything but the truth. However "orthodox" you may desire to be, "God's orthodoxy is truth."

In the Old Testament men did not always with justice interpret the movement of the Divine Spirit in their hearts, as in that terrible commission of slaughter, when Samuel mistook patriotic passion for Divine fire. And in the New Testament Apostles made mistakes: Paul withstood Peter— which was right? Peter, at first, believed he was right in abstaining from Gentile fellowship; afterwards he corrected his error. Many disciples, along with Paul and the Thessalonians, were mistaken about Christ's early return; and within certain limits it may be asserted that Christendom was founded on that illusion.

What, then, does all this

prove ? Simply that God does not reject the fallibility of men as an unfit vehicle of His inspiration. "Holy men spoke as they were moved by the Holy Ghost," but they were not, because inspired, thereby qualified to pass an examination in all things in Heaven and Earth, past, present, and to come.

Believe me, the rest in final authoritative teaching is but temporary and delusive; the next stage is atheism and despair. I love and trust the Bible too much to protect it with any *chevaux de frise.* This Book is the classic of religion, speaking in many tones; I hold it to be the charter of the freedom and progress of man, the record of the Word of God, His gift to us. Read it carefully and prayerfully. Its light shines from God. Rich with the spoils of time, its worth is not less but greater as the generations pass.

Let the truth be found, if God permit. And, when it is found, let it be published abroad, as God assuredly wills. For truth is His ally, "fair as the morn, clear as the sun, and terrible as an army with banners."

V.

POSITIVE RESULTS OF
THE HIGHER CRITICISM.

POSITIVE RESULTS OF THE HIGHER CRITICISM.

"Ye search the Scriptures, because ye think that in them ye have eternal life; and these are they which bear witness of me."—St. John v. 39.

I TRUST you will not suppose that the Higher Criticism is a term of self-praise adopted by supercilious scholars. The sciolist, who condemns it on that account, resembles the gentleman of reactionary tendencies, who, in be-rating his contemporaries, said, "This nineteenth century"! and then with withering scorn, "This so-called nineteenth century"!

The higher or historic criticism is simply a name that distinguishes it from the lower, or grammatical and textual, criticism. The former explores with ampler method and farther reaching purposes, attempts to learn the truth about the origin of the books, the circumstances that gave rise to them, the motives that directed their writers. The mineralogist analyses the composition of the rocks, the geologist explores the stratification of the earth's surface, and systematises the results of minuter observations. This is the larger function of the Higher Criticism. We are familiar enough with its results in other fields. Greek history has been, in recent years, traced in firmer outline than was possible to Plato himself; of Roman history we have a surer grasp than had Cicero; and similarly the history and religion of the Hebrews are seen more clearly to-day by those who will avail themselves of the best results to hand, than by the men who collected and canonised the Old Testament or the rabbis of Jewry.

In speaking of the positive results of the Higher Criticism, I fear that, inadequate as has been my treatment of the foregoing subjects, the present attempt must be, in the nature of things, still more unsatisfactory. But there is this consolatory reflection, that the whole of my ministry is positive, and that it is my continual delight to fasten your attention on the great foundation truths of the Gospel of Christ for the need of man. Now I want to suggest to you that the Higher Criticism is the honest attempt of our best scholars to *save the Bible.* I want to make you feel sure that just as the net result of the negative attack on the Gospel is that it has tightened its hold upon society, so the net result of the most fearless Biblical criticism is that the Bible is made a more capable instrument of religious education and spiritual culture.

Some of the most striking results of recent Biblical criticism are undoubtedly negative in their character so far as the general public is concerned. The demolition is the more dramatic, and, at first, monopolises the attention, so that only students see the possibility and promise of constructive work. At first its influence is rather discomposing than invigorating to one's beliefs, but one can hardly expect to build a new house on the site of the old without some little temporary disturbance.

The loss is much more apparent than real. We lose an impracticable, misleading theory of no edifying value whatever. We do not lose the

Scriptures, nor one grain of their profitableness for instruction in righteousness. We lose some cherished prepossessions along with that shadowy fetish —say, rather, we lose a heavy burden and grievous to be borne, and with it a crowd of difficulties. We gain a more reasonable ground for faith and a more enlightened assurance of the continuity of the Divine redeeming purpose. While the dawn is young a little sunshine raises the mists, but more sunshine dispels them. Let us have enough confidence in Christianity to believe that no criticism can do it harm ; it is indeed a fragile thing if it be endangered by examination of its own evidence. I believe that the Bible is not merely as much as before, but that it is much more than it ever was. The tearing away of old associations is distressing and painful ;

the pruning-knife of criticism
cuts deep, but it cuts well, nor
is there any danger in the knife
of truth, save to the growth of
error and superstition. To say
otherwise, nay, to think otherwise, means infidelity, all the
more dark and subtle because
it does not recognise itself for
what it is—fear of the truth
and doubt of the God of truth.
Oh for more faith in God !

> All is well, tho' faith and form
>   Be sundered in the night of fear,
>   Well roars the storm to those that hear
> A deeper voice across the storm.

For pity's sake let us not be
such slaves of circumstance as
to imagine that the sole crite-
rion of truth is its immediate
utility. Were it of no gain
at all, still the true thing must
be spoken, yes, even though it
should seem to destroy what
men call an essential. "Essential " for what ? Nothing

short of the truth can be essential for the best life of the soul of a child of God.

If you have followed me at all sympathetically up to this point, you will see that we are relieved from the responsibility and unthankful office of apologising for God by trying to explain away the crudities of the earlier pages of the Bible. The doings of Jacob and the sins of David were not recorded for our approval but for our disapproval and instruction. The slaughter of the Canaanites was largely a fancy picture painted to encourage an intolerant spirit of patriotism. If, indeed, God had been such as He is here at times portrayed, we might justly have said with Prometheus, "I reverence Thee —wherefore?" Great gain has thus been made for intellectual candour. The man who any longer imagines that all the

Biblical content is the smooth, uniform utterance of the Divine mind, and that every Hebrew " Thus saith the Lord " is the indisputable oracle of the Almighty Father, has a pathetic intellectual simplicity.   Our fathers, in their disputes, frequently said that one clear text is as good as a thousand, no matter from what quarter of the Bible it has been drawn.   They did not hesitate to build the most portentous inferences upon the most slender textual foundation ; indeed, they delighted in what Coleridge called " the ever-widening spiral *ergo* out of the narrow aperture of single texts." We have acquired a sense of proportion and perspective.   We want to know when, where, by whom and under what circumstances the text originated ; for we are aware that there is in the Bible increasing and improving knowledge of what is truly Divine as the Book moves on. The ideas that the people cherished in early days were denounced by the prophets as foolishness, and by Christ as little more than ignorance. There is a prayer in the Psalms (cix.) that the writer's enemy may be cursed of God, his days few, his wife a widow, and his children fatherless vagabonds on whom none will have mercy. There is another prayer (Psalm cxxxvii.), "Happy shall he be who taketh and dasheth thy little ones against the rock." If those verses are inspired, by whom are they inspired but by the spirit of all evil ? Some ancient texts are merely fossils, which are useful enough for studying past development, but, though of animal origin, are scarcely available for digestion as food. Through a whole wilderness of mistakes and crudities and delusions lay the way of the Bible towards its final goal —first the natural, after that the spiritual. Do not rack your brain and strain your conscience in the attempt to accept what your moral sense rejects. It would be strange if, after the illumining influence of Christ, you did not find imperfections in the low levels of early thought and life.

We have gained a credible clue to the origin and history of the Canonical books. By means of the introduction of a more correct historic perspective, we see that every part has its own immediate and local meaning. The men of the Bible are kindred souls of like passions with ourselves; there is living movement and human reality in the pages. Is there a man for whom the Bible is less real and powerful because it was not written by denaturalised

men, with the pen of angels,
but fashioned by the experiences of human life, and toned
by the varying moods of human
souls, now tremulous with re-
morse and heart-break, now
glad with victorious faith ?

For us, the worth of the
Hebrew Scriptures begins with
the fact that ancient Israel was
the first people of the world to
see that religiousness and goodness are essentially one. In the
old world, familiar to us through
many channels, the religious
man needed not to be a good
man. Why should he be ? The
gods were often vile, so vile,
that to be manlike was better
than to be godlike. To the
modern man godliness is one
with goodness; to the ancient
godliness was often viciousness.
Now, it was a transcendent
moment when there entered the
heart of man the great idea that
God and Righteousness are

really and everlastingly one.
In that moment Religion began
to mean, before all else, morality
and the service of God; to
mean, before all else, the doing
of duty to men. That was a
moment of Revelation. " Be ye
holy, for I am holy, saith your
God." Through Moses that
signal service was rendered to
his people ; he bound them, by
religion, to righteousness. By
that discovery he laid the foundation of that nation in the
Holy One of Israel. That was
the Law of Moses in its essence.
All the Law grew from that
germ, and subsequent additions
through the long centuries were
quite naturally connected with
the name, and invested with the
authority, of the great Lawgiver
of Israel. Robertson Smith com-
pared it with the supposition or
legal fiction of Roman Juris-
prudence, whereby all law was
supposed to be derived from the

Laws of the Twelve Tables. No falsehood was meant or conveyed. The object was to maintain the continuity of the legal system.

In the same way the Psalter was connected with David, the "sweet singer of Israel." Like Moses, he embodied an influence and a tendency; he was the centre around which the poetry of the nation crystallised, as did the Law round Moses. Not that nearly all the Psalms were written by him. Far otherwise. They were the voice, not of one man, but of the great congregation. They are in five sections (1-41, 42-72, 73-89, 90-106, 107-150), and each section ends with a doxology, after the pious Oriental fashion. And if there is any one who, at the first blush, regrets their dissociation from David, and is tempted to regard that as a grievous loss, I would suggest to him this ques-

tion : Would the Book of
Common Prayer be of more
value if it fell out that Henry
the Eighth was its sole author ?
It is well to remember that
traditional criticism of the long
ago was prone to ascribe as
many books as possible to pro-
minent names, Moses, David,
Solomon ; modern criticism has
had to distribute them to their
proper, even if unknown,
authorship.

The prophets too, under simi-
lar freedom of treatment, are
made actually accessible and
comprehensible. According to
a widespread method of
thought, there are large tracts
of the Old Testament which do
not mean anything in particu-
lar, and were not intended to
mean much. For the average
man of the pew the prophecies
are closed, or, if open, only as a
museum of antiquities, which
" visitors are requested not to

touch." The Higher Criticism
has shed such light on the
prophecies that they are made
"habitable by modern men," interesting to students of history,
and intelligible to thoughtful
religious people. They have
been the lone hunting-ground
of millenarians and others,
who regarded them as the riddles of sacred weather - prophets. In being made a branch
of Christian evidence they have
been impoverished. They are
being reclaimed for civilised
uses. The Book of Daniel,
for instance, was written in
the second century B.C., in a
time of Israel's deep depression.
It was the expression of her
passionate revolt against the
tyranny of Antiochus Epi-
phanes; it was the Gospel of
that age, and kept alive the
vital spark of a people in a
crucial hour, when it was just
possible that Israel might have

gone out without producing Christianity. That prophecy was no forecast of modern European political changes. The predictive element in prophecy has been unduly magnified by the popular imagination. Why, the distinction of a true prophet was that he was no soothsayer; that *rôle* he scornfully left to the false prophets, and when he did, as rarely, indulge in prediction he was frequently wrong (Isaiah xxiii. Jeremiah xxxvi. 30. Amos vii. 10—17). So far as the ideal moral order, which they predicated, is carried out by events, so far their prevision was justified by results; in proportion as history swerves from the ideal moral order, so far they were mistaken. They felt after tendencies, and sometimes their predictions were strangely fulfilled; but they "understood in part." The prophets were

men who got behind tradition to
reality, behind the expediencies
of the moment to the just thing
that stands in the power of God ;
they were reformers amidst the
strife, men of insight and conviction, of a vision and a faculty
Divine, who saw life steadily
and saw it whole, and therefore
bade their comrades face the
future without fear. " God
must fulfil Himself," said they.
" His promises are the impera-
tive of His nature ; it must be
so." Thoughts beyond their
thought to those high bards
were given, and with resolute
hand they held aloft the torch
of hope, lit by the sun of the
better day that was coming.
" Instead (says Pfleiderer) of
having in Hebrew history a
series of riddles, of psychologi-
cal and historical puzzles,
everything is comprehensible.
We have a clear development,
analogous to the rest of history,

the external history of the
nation and the internal history
of its religious consciousness in
constant accord and fruitful
intercourse, and though not an
unbroken advance in a straight
line of the whole people, still a
laborious struggle of the repre-
sentatives of the highest truth
with the stolid masses, a struggle in which success and defeat
succeed each other in dramatic
alternation, and even failure
only seems to aid the evolution
of the idea itself in even
greater purity from its original
integuments. This is human
history, full of marvels and of
Divine Revelation, but nowhere
interrupted by miracle or by
sudden unaccountable transi-
tions." Revelation depends always on man's power to see,
not on God's willingness to
reveal. God reveals Himself
whenever we learn more of His
truth.

Then, not only is the Bible made more comprehensible, but the apologetic power of the Bible is increased. The old secularist attacks on the book become ridiculous, when it is seen that their weapons are out of date and innocuous, and their gibes without point. The most popular anti-Christian tract in our day is the " Mistakes of Moses." It was written in the worst possible taste, so that many of you doubtless shrank from reading it ; but its main contention was justified, as long as the average Christian argued that if Moses made a mistake all religion was a falsity, and there was a summary end of Christian faith and hope for this world and the next. It and its congeners had some force as a protest against such a notion of the Bible as we know to be unfounded. It was the theory that provoked

attack; men disbelieved with
defiance, as under a sense of
attempted wrong and trium-
phant escape. "Here are blem-
ishes," they said; "absurd science and contradictory stories,
predatory wars and barbarous
laws; *that* is the morality of
your infallible book." As well
judge a sculptor by a fragment
of broken stone in his studio.
Those things were not the end
towards which progressive Revelation was moving. That is
not the morality of the Bible.
Remember the dominating and
persevering tendency which
is the vital spirit of the
Bible. How did Israelitism
work out? Did it overcome the
crudities and extrude them?
Only children and fools judge
things as they appear; wise
men try to discern things as
they are. As well treat the
sky as a flat vault, neglecting
all the depth of heaven and

the incalculable distance of the stars, and forgetting all the astronomy you ever knew, as treat this volume, full of thousands of years, as if it had all been written yesterday, without any historic perspective at all. Like the old world itself the Bible was long a-growing.

Some have been grieved because of some things I have ventured to say, but these Philistine attacks upon the sacred legacy of the past move me (as one bred on the Bible and loving it dearly) to scornful wonder. Who are we, in these late days of debt to that long past, that, like imps of mischief, we should push out lips of mocking laughter at the painful upward struggle of the dead centuries, at the poor, pathetic mistakes made by men whose experiences generated the religious atmosphere that we breathe ? It is as unfair as it is graceless. These ancient Scriptures must be assayed, not beside sheets fresh from Paternoster-row, but beside the awful immorality and unspeakable religions of contemporary peoples. In no ancient state was the idea of God so imperial and majestic, so kindly and tender; in none was man so dignified, or life so lofty. Their laws were humane to the men who toiled, their literature was deeply compassionate to the poor, their most sacred sanctions threw a shield of defence over the weak, and nobly vindicated the cause of the oppressed. Grant that we are driven to deny the perfectness of their conceptions; at least let us remember that if we are enabled to correct their moral mistakes, it is the Bible itself that supplies the standard which we employ.

That people which was always

turning back, was perpetually pressed forward along the highway of the Lord, as by an inevitable force, towards their destiny. What is this goal towards which the Scriptures moved? What is this standard of perfection by which we judge? Christ, the Word of God, to whom the whole book turns, of whom it is the record, in whom it culminates. The history of Israel is the time-development of the Christ; "God, who at sundry times and in divers manners spake by the prophets, hath spoken to us by His Son." Letter by letter He taught His people, until, in the fulness of time, He gave the Word which from the beginning was God.

It has been said that all Biblical criticism finally resolves itself into questions about Christ; the Higher Criticism accentuates that truth as it has never been accentuated before. Behold the Man ! Behold the Lamb of God ! He is the Master—He, so long overshadowed by the Bibliolatry which dared to say, " By me, if any man enter in he shall be saved !" He is the Servant of God of whom the prophets bare witness, the Messiah of Humanity, the God-man. He is the Saviour of the world, a quickening Spirit who betters us, we know not how, who binds us to the love of virtue, and communicates His Spirit in perpetual possession. Under the play of historical criticism the figure of Christ has drawn nearer us and stands in clearer light.

That one face, far from vanish, rather grows,
Or decomposes but to recompose,
Becomes my Universe that feels and knows.

Under the light of historical criticism the Bible is seen to be the long way to the Christ, Immanuel, our human Brother and Friend; that was the increasing purpose that ran through the ages, and "The veil was done away in Christ." The time-honoured maxim of Chillingworth, "The Bible only the Religion of Protestants," is superseded by the better maxim, "Christ only the Religion of Christians."

Men have been patching motley texts together and "proving things," constructing systems and rearing prodigious theories about things celestial and things terrestrial; but unless the Bible leads their souls to Christ, the Master and Saviour of all souls, they search the Scriptures in vain. The text which I have chosen for this evening was long read as if Jesus had been exhorting the Pharisees to search the Scriptures: they did little else.

They thought that they knew
and understood the Scriptures
above all others; they wor-
shipped the law and the testimony. This, rather, was what
Christ said : " Ye search the
Scriptures, and in *them* ye think
ye have eternal life; you miss
their best meaning, you are
blind to their ultimate purpose,
—they testify of Me,—I am the
Light of the world,—I am He
of whom Moses did write."
And by the new emphasis that
is laid by the Higher Criticism
upon the person and authority
of our Lord, a signal service is
rendered to the cause of true
religion. Loyalty to Him is the
one test of Christian life, and
in closer apprehension of the
truth as it is in Jesus lies the
only hope of real union among
men who profess and call themselves Christians.

I am well aware that the main
question will be decided, not by

critical dissertation, but the consideration of the improvement, the gain that these innovations bring along with them. The plain man wants to know— "Does the Bible become more intelligible? Will the new arrangement produce a cosmos or a chaos?" The answer to that question is the verdict on the whole. The Higher Criticism, by intensifying the human and literary interest of the Bible, is likely to multiply its students and readers. It is doing so, and not before it was needed, for the Bible has shared the fate of most classics—to be more talked about than read. It has been so long viewed as a treasury of texts or a quarry of oracles that its intellectual interest was, for many people, occasionally at vanishing point. To its misfortune it is the volume from which the preachers extract their texts ; and to its greater misfortune, the people who read it most regularly read it in textual snippets. How is it possible under such a method to appreciate the majesty of the Book, the breadth of its horizon, the largeness of its spirit? How many of us have so much as thought of reading through and mastering even the shortest book of all the sixty-six—to catch its real drift and purport? That great artist in letters, of whose lonely burial in the southern sea we have this week learnt, once wrote, "I believe it would startle and move any one, if they could make a certain effort of imagination, if they could read the Gospel according to St. Matthew freshly like a book, not droningly and dully like a portion of the Bible." Of course, we are all tolerably familiar with those parts of the Bible which are included in the formal and informal lectionaries of the churches, and by courtesy we are supposed to know the whole volume intimately. But so desultory is our reading, and for the most part superficial, that, in truth, the sacred volume holds a dark continent unexplored by most of us. The Higher Criticism, in adding to the literary, historic, and moral worth of the Bible, makes the whole of the book vividly interesting, and some of the least regarded portions, apparently sterile and uninviting, are now most fascinating. So much is this the case that I fully anticipate a renaissance of Bible - reading among the people, as it is gradually understood that the best book for the heart has been made the best book for the intellect too, and that our paramount instrument for devotion and heartsease is equally paramount as a

means of liberal intellectual
education.

Of course, remembering how
the Bible fixes our thoughts
steadily on the bettering of
character, we must never forget that a man can draw practical benefit from the Bible
without any theory whatever,
just as the light of day is
sweet, whether we understand
the undulatory hypothesis or
not. The helpfulness and vi-
tality stored in these written
words is marvellous beyond all
telling, and I will not make
the old, melancholy, and mischievous mistake of supposing
that any theory is indispensable
to Christianity. No ; a man
can be a good Christian into
whatever mould he runs his
intellectual conclusions. "The
light that never was on sea or
land" does not depend, for the
clearness of its shining, on the
correctness of our premises and

analyses. But I am not asking
how little use and understanding of the Bible is compatible
with Christian culture ; my
anxiety is rather to increase
our use and deepen our understanding of it. Surely it is good
to know what demonstrable
truth we may about this Divine
Library, which wields an influence like nothing else, reveals us to ourselves, and more
than all else reveals to us the
communing and redeeming
Presence of our God and
Father. Its beauties and de-
lights increase as we the more
understand it. No criticism
can hope to explain the Bible
completely, any more than
chemistry or physiology can
explain a man. But the might
and majesty of the Book are
made more conspicuous, and
its serviceableness is increased ;
it is made more " profitable for
doctrine, for reproof, for correc-

tion, for instruction in righteousness," while its place is
made more impregnable than
ever before. It is our book of
Religion, inextricably one with
our highest hopes, one with our
fathers' prayers and all the
yearnings of the Christian ages.
Its words have a glow and a
force which belong to no other
Book. Guarded by the love of
mankind, it stands, the promise
and potency of God's tender
care for the souls of men, and
under its shadow we go to that
fair day in which " The Lord
God Himself giveth them light
for ever."

LONDON:
W. SPEAIGHT AND SONS, PRINTERS,
FETTER LANE.

www.ingramcontent.com/pod-product-compliance
Lightning Source LLC
Chambersburg PA
CBHW020232030726
47497CB00009B/3063